FRUITBAT

A Novella Remix

Dear Readers …

Let me (re)introduce myself. I'm Michael Easton Star. Some of you knew me as Micah Carver—in a previous embodiment. I've been writing since age eleven, with a significant pause for several tears, before coming back to this beloved craft in 2023.

I published a handful of novels as "Micah" in 2024, but felt it was time for an authentic remix. "FRUITBAT" was my third piece and I never felt it was given the level of magic I really wanted it to have. The story has been remixed and I am launching it into the world as it was intended to be.

All my love and appreciation,

MICHAEL EASTON STAR

CONTENTS

1

10:32 PM

SI FLOATS RAPTLY ON smooth undulating waves of music. The songstress pleads for her lover *not* to prove her right. *But they always do, don't they?* He notions and chuffs—swaying in the symphonic current—desperate for rhythmic tides to carry the day away. Swallowed up in a resonant bubble, drowning out the surging sea of his friends, and their friends.

His knees bow, and his hips writhe side to side, as he raises both arms overhead—like a creature caught in a net, trying to wriggle free. He lays his head back, surrendering to the melody, while he sinks into a whirlpool of costumed characters dancing around him.

His building-mates insisted on throwing this *"Slasher Bash,"* to celebrate Halloween, inviting only the most coveted contacts in their collective lists. The vapid pair love exploiting any opportunity to boost their social relevance.

As usual, Si's apartment became the party's central hub. It wasn't his idea, but he didn't protest when he had the chance.

He enjoys the euphoria of being surrounded by community—from time to time. Even when the connections aren't genuine.

It's also exhausting.

Not one so-called *friend* at this party has remembered it is also his day. The 30th anniversary of a person's birth should be a pivotal point in one's life, but he's not feeling like it.

Mallory—the *best of* his *best* friends—lives in the third-floor apartment. Her birthday is just two days away. She'd been dropping not-so-subtle hints at her own curated gift list for weeks, all the while making no recognition of Si's day.

He got her the slouchy cream cashmere sweater from her favorite boutique up the street. She'd practically assigned him the task.

Eager to please, he's always the one left disappointed.

Sharing his birthday with the beloved holiday goes down the same way every year. He hopes for "Happy Birthday" wishes that never come, but no one ever forgets to cheer "Happy Halloween."

When he was a child, Nanny Grace used to remind everyone—including his parents. She raised him and his four siblings, dedicating more of her life to them than her own two children. While Si's Mother and Father jetted around the globe.

She'd been the one person he could count on, until she passed away when he was thirteen. He's been forgotten ever since. It's unfathomable to him how people forget important dates so easily. He could never.

"Si!" Damien calls out. His voice is muffled—light years away.

Si carries on, ebbing and flowing to the music.

"Hey—Josiah!" Damien shouts in his ear. He clamps a hand onto Si's shoulder, reeling him back from the musical trance.

"Yeah?" Si shouts back. He pauses, edged with frustration, as his bubble pops.

"Did you get tequila?" Damien bellows.

His rancid beer breath is hot on Si's cheek, and black dilated pupils consume his eyes, rimmed thinly with blood-red irises.

"Those contacts are so creepy." Si says, grimacing.

"That's the point." Damien responds, cackling.

His black hair is slicked back with gel, and his face is powdered white. A drip of crimson corn-syrup trails the edge of his mouth, dry and crackling down his chin.

"The tequila is in my room," Si says. "I'll get it." He twirls his index finger in the air and steps into the horde, adding, "One sec."

Damien sucks on his plastic fangs and melts back into the crowd, bopping along to the beat.

Damien, Mallory, and Si have known each other since they were kindergarteners, attending the fancy private academy their parents had enrolled them in. The adults forced the trio to socialize, while they hobnobbed in pretentious circles.

Si is sure his *besties* would have nothing to do with him if his father were not the prestigious lawyer and real estate moonlighter, which he is.

The impromptu host weaves through the crowd, up the hall, stopping at the bathroom door, desperate to relieve himself of the four vodka-cranberries he's consumed.

A boisterous trio of ladies—that he barely recognizes—stumbles out, laughing and poking at each other. Barbie in neon rollerskating gear, a platinum-wigged black cat in a negligee, and Patrick Star, swiping white powder from her nostril on the backside of her pointy sleeve.

Si flattens himself against the wall to let them pass, and quickly locks himself into the toilet. Sharing the room with a skunky cloud of smoke as he does his business.

He sneers at the mirror for reflecting a frazzled blond nest of curls, sallow-gray skin, and smeared black-shadow rimmed eyes. A week-long binge, consuming episodes of *The Walking Dead,* had inspired the zombie costume.

With a quick shrug of his shoulder, and sucking in, he pats his exposed belly. The chewed-up crop-top is the crowning glory of his handmade costume. A tinge of slut-tified edge is key to any respectable gay's Halloween attire.

Si slips out of the bathroom and weaves up the hall, into his bedroom. Quickly latching the door shut, he leans back against it and releases a heavy exhale.

The room is an intoxicating refuge—or he's just floating on a contact high. He collects the two bottles of tequila from his computer desk and sets them outside the door, before barricading himself away with a turn of the lock.

He's done with the party for the rest of the night.

A chilly draft creeps in under the cracked-open window, carrying fleeting voices in conversation from the street outside.

Si crosses the room and hauls the window wide open. He slinks out onto the fire escape, closes his eyes, and pulls a long draw of autumn air in his nostrils. Hoping to sober his sloshing mind.

Wrought iron clanks and moans as he descends into the dark alleyway.

The abandoned street is barely lit by a sparse scattering of streetlamps. He briefly looks back up at the window of his second-floor apartment—sandwiched between Damien and Mallory's dwellings. Then proceeds around the corner.

He's been walking this same trek every night for several weeks—doctor's orders—to relieve a recent bout of anxiety and cure his insomnia.

Knotting his goose-pimpling arms around his bare waist—wishing he'd grabbed a sweater—he meanders toward the park. *Exertion will warm me up soon enough,* he figures.

The city park is framed by a split-rail fence, which he hurdles over, and trots along the crushed gravel path. Stones pop under the rubber soles of his sneakers.

Distant voices chatter, but move away.

The forested oasis is a sweet escape from the urban chaos when you venture deep enough, especially after dark.

A new moon hangs brightly in the sky, spreading the looming shadows of naked trees across the ground. Petrified leaves flit over gravel paths on whispering winds, escaping the piles left behind by landscaping crews.

A pair of raccoons rummaging in trash bins glowers at the intruder.

Si hurries past their territory, glancing back to appreciate the fluffy ringed tails flailing over the tops of the steel cans.

"Too cute," he whispers, chuckling.

Typically, Si veers left at the fork in the path, then loops back home, to climb into bed. But tonight he turns right. Knowing the party will carry until daylight. He's in no rush to return.

This alternate route leads to a bridge that crosses over the river, to the *grittier* half of the city.

Up ahead, a festive pack of monsters and ghouls crowds around a park bench. Their beastly werewolf leader is re-enacting some splendid tale that has the group cackling like a clan of hyenas.

Si nearly turns back, but cautiously strolls forward, trying to carry himself confidently.

As he approaches, their gossip simmers, and they all turn with foreboding faces.

A shiver wiggles through him, but he offers a nervous grin, hoping they're friendly.

The crew are in their late teens or early twenties; he can't tell anymore. At his new age, young people all look the same, and they're all intimidating.

Si swallows the hard lump in his throat and gurgles, "Hey." Forcing a smile.

"Hey," the flanneled furry pack leader responds, studying Si with narrow eyes.

The curious clan all stare at him, up and down, until he passes by.

Hold it together, *Si,* he encourages himself.

Their cackles commence once he's reached a reasonable distance.

Si squeezes a heavy breath out of his gut and drops his shoulders with relief. He carries on through the park and hurdles the fence on the far side.

A wide stretch of highway is clear when he checks both directions before stepping into the crosswalk.

The bridge is straight ahead, and the other side of the city is just past the river. It babbles and shimmers with moonlit sequins.

Squealing tires and headlights suddenly sweep the pavement, interrupting his quiet stroll.

Si turns toward the commotion.

A dark SUV with blackout windows rips around the corner, and barrels straight toward him. Its LED bulbs are blinding, and its screeching tires echo over the river.

Si freezes in the middle of the street, clenching his eyes, bracing for impact, but his body jumps into autopilot. He launches off the ground, tucks into a somersault, and rolls over the pavement. His shoulder crashes against the center median curb.

"Ouch!" he hollers.

The monstrous truck's engine roars and its wheels sear the pavement with blood-curdling wails. It reclaims its speed hastily and tears down the street.

"Asshole!" Si screams as he stands up and brushes debris off his body.

Tail lights taunt him as they trail away into the night.

Si trembles and clutches his chest. His head spins as he tries to catch his breath.

"What the fu—" he wheezes, swallowing his insides back down to where they belong. He swipes a bead of sweat from his brow and shakes off the terrifying moment. Then collects himself, as best he can, and carries on.

This half of the city smells different, bizarrely sweet. It reminds him of Grace baking treats in the oven while he observed from the breakfast nook. The memory eases his anxiety.

Trees are sparse and withered on this side of the river. It's mostly old brick, concrete, and depression. The buildings are decorated with graffiti. Some are charming; some, not so much. Bits of trash scatter the edges of the streets, and flit across pavement, like the leaves in the park, but less ethereal.

His mother and her privileged cohorts from Park Row would *never* let this fly in *their* neighborhood. Once, they chewed the mayor a new one—over brunch—after finding a loose candy bar wrapper on the sidewalk.

Si giggles at the vision of his mother's face, if she were to see the state of this side of *her* city. Though he's sure there will be more prominent traffic lights at that intersection when she hears about his encounter.

It'll give her pretentious pride of lionesses something to roar about.

2

10:59 PM

DANNY

A REPULSIVE BELL CHIMES as Danny flings the door open, announcing his arrival and triggering a twitch in his brow. He steps through the steel-framed glass storefront, letting the door close itself. It expels a peeved sigh before old hydraulic hinges quit, and it slams shut behind him.

Same door—same, he sympathizes.

A sour stench of ammoniated lemon stings his sinuses, and the barely audible hum of harsh fluorescent lights causes his jaw to clench.

This place makes his skin crawl.

Danny has worked the nightmare shift, in this hellhole convenience store for four years now. He's not sure food and shelter are really worth the hassle, but his dreams of making it in the literary world have yet to manifest.

Of course, it would help if he'd finally write a new piece this decade.

The tattered messenger bag, slung across his body, carries the fruitless manuscripts—taking up megabytes in his barely functioning laptop—that every agent and publisher that's ever seen them has rejected.

"Hey Danny," Delila says cheerily.

How is she always so fucking perky? Danny grumbles. *It's 11 0'clock for* fuck's *sake,* he thinks, while he marches toward the office.

Her bubbly personality shouldn't irk him the way it does. It's the end of her shift, and she's likely just happy he showed up again, so she can go home. They've never worked together, only passed in the night, when shifts change over.

"Hey," Danny says. Pandering a half smile. He rubs his cheek to soothe the sore muscle after performing the forced expression.

"I like your shirt." Delila says, beaming with far too much enthusiasm.

"Thanks," Danny responds. He peers down at the once-black, now faded old tee with the ghostly decal of a band logo—so shattered it looks like bits of paper went through the wash and he couldn't be bothered to peel them off.

Delila always makes a complimentary remark.

Danny wonders what it must be like to exist so positively in this cruel world.

Delila tears open a box of chocolate bars. "I'll leave these for you—the shelf needs restocking," she says, slipping two bars into her pocket, while tilting her shoulder up to block the security camera's view.

Danny rolls his eyes and chuckles.

This place doesn't pay enough to afford anything above basic necessities. The staff collect their own little bonuses from time to time. It's not likely anyone will ever check the footage.

Danny doesn't even bother with discretion anymore. Nobody has been fired yet.

The new owner is probably using the place for some shady money-laundering scheme. No one on the crew has met them. It's supposedly some moonlighting entrepreneur with more capital than they know what to do with.

The missing goods probably help them cook their books, anyway.

Danny's supposed to manage inventory checks, but he's not done that for at-least two years.

"Okay—it'll give me something to do." Danny says as he scoots past Delila and slips into the office to drop his bag on the folding chair, and clock in.

The archaic machine hanging on the wall sears a barely legible 10:59 onto the yellow strip of cardstock.

Right on time. Danny sneers.

Delila pops her head through the doorway and punches her card before he's even stepped out of the way. She smells of sour pickles—her favorite snack, according to the empty jars she leaves about every night—and cheap fruity shampoo. Not the gag-inducing combination you'd imagine. It's reminiscent of the deceptive kombucha drinks in the fridge at the back of the store. They smell okay, but taste rancid.

Delila gathers up her things, and slips into a short-waisted, shiny-lavender quilted jacket. Her thick berry-flavored corkscrew curls are swept up into a twisted knot atop her head.

Danny envies her creamy brown skin. A lack of exposure to daylight these past few years has left him pale as a ghost. He doesn't have much reason to leave his tiny studio apartment after he gets home, just past dawn. He spends his days sleeping, and he spends his nights working.

Once upon a time, he savored the peaceful bliss of night—before he took on this fucking gig. He thought it would allow him the time and space to write—while collecting an actual paycheck—but he usually stares at a blank screen and blinking cursor. Then, instead, trolls random internet forums until the end of his shifts.

"Have a good one," Delila says. She loops the strap of her glittery purple purse across her chest and wedges it tight against her hip. "Happy Halloween," she adds.

"Oh, yeah—you too." Danny replies. He had forgotten what day it was, although the city had been decorated for weeks. He'd slept through any potential trick-or-treaters. Not that anyone was climbing three floors inside the sketchy walk-up where he lives. He wouldn't bother answering if they did.

The repulsive bell chimes again as Delila struts outside, and down the sidewalk, before the door slams shut.

Danny's teeth clench, and he closes his eyes for a moment of meditation. He could probably just lock up and go home, then come back in the morning for the shift switch, with no one noticing. But, *fuck it,* he's already here.

He flips open the spout of a tall silver thermos, lined-up along the wall with its brethren, and fills a paper cup with dark roast brew. Then stands at the center of the room, facing up to the camera, while he blows ripples across the black sludge's surface, and slurps. His eyes narrow in a glare at big brother's lense, challenging the tiny red pin-light beaming down at him.

He suppresses the urge to flip his middle finger up at the camera, because it doesn't deserve that.

Danny winces with disgust, realizing the coffee is probably from the same batch that has sat all day. Most likely even the same pot he had brewed from last night, that still hasn't been changed.

He spits it back into the cup, and spins around on his heel, then stomps toward the sink at the back of the store.

The place is grossly familiar. Nothing ever changes. Shelves take months, even years, to empty and just get refilled with expired junk from the moldy storage room in the basement. Some of the garbage has probably sat here longer than he's been an employee. Thick layers of dust prove that theory.

He rounds the grocery shelf, into the farthest aisle, but his footing doesn't quite contact the floor, and his foot slips out from under him. His right heel glides over some slick barrier coating the tile and his arms flail, reaching for a plastic barrel end-cap—which should be full of hard ciders—hoping to catch himself, but it tumbles sideways, under his weight, and he pulls it down with his fall.

Danny's head bashes against the sharp corner of a steel shelving unit, and his breath catches, before the world blurs into a spiraling dark tunnel.

3

11:11 PM

"Oh, no!" Si blurts and bolts forward. His legs carry him swiftly, floating over pavement, leaping onto the sidewalk across the street. A bell chimes as he storms through the storefront and scurries to the fallen clerk's side.

The poor guy is sprawled out on the floor, soaking up a soapy puddle.

Si witnessed the slip after pausing his trek to peep through the store windows. The show was comical at first, like viewing an actor flailing over-the-top in one of those vintage silent films. But then he smashed his head on the metal shelf. Si could feel the impact in his own skull, which cracked in solidarity.

"Shit," Si whispers. *He's out cold.* He panics and reaches into his pocket to collect his phone. But he must have left it at home. "Dammit," he mutters. His sneakers struggle to grip the slick floor as he pulls himself up and skates toward the checkout counter.

He hops up, lays his bare belly on the linoleum, and leans over the cash register. His eyes scan the wall of booze and cigarettes, then drop below, to the cubby compartments behind the counter, but there's no phone.

He skids around the counter, through an open doorway, and into a small office. Noticing the tattered messenger bag draped over the chair. "This must be his," he guesses. Scooping it up and rummaging through its pockets.

Si's fingers search, but only find an old laptop, a bundle of manila folders packed with papers, several pens that clink against a tube of chapstick, and the recognizable shape of an asthmatic's inhaler. Damien keeps them all over their building in case of emergencies.

He tucks the little device into his pocket, and scurries back out to the unconscious clerk.

Kneeling at his side. Si folds down, hovering his cheek over the stranger's chest, and notes the rise and fall of his breaths. "That's good," he assures himself.

The stranger's soft belly peeks out from beneath the hem of his faded t-shirt. His thick arms sprawl out over the floor. His shaggy dark hair is clipped tight at the sides, forming a choppy mullet of sorts, and it is drenched in mop water.

Si twists around, spotting rolls of paper towel lining the shelf. He crawls through the soapy puddle, grabs a roll, and tears it open. He wraps his arm in several sheets, tucks the rolls under his elbow, and shimmies back to the fallen man, wiping up the surrounding floor.

He gathers a second roll to clean himself up. Wrinkling his nose at the acidic scent. Unsure what more to do, he settles back against a shelf and pulls his knees up to his chest. Waiting. Watching over the stranger until he stirs and groans.

Si readies the inhaler, rolls back up, and crawls to the clerk's side.

His dark brown eyes flicker open, and squint.

Si hovers over his face to block out the harsh fluorescent lights. "Hey," he says, with a tender smile.

4

11:27 PM

DANNY

"WHAT THE ..." DANNY mumbles. He shakes his head to focus his blurry eyes on the ghoulish blond hanging over him.

He studies the buttery curls, mangled and poking out in all directions. Hazel eyes, ringed in dark circles, and skin the color of spoiled chicken. A fluorescent halo from the buzzing lights surrounds him.

"Don't get up," the zombie says.

Danny scrambles up on his hands and scoots backward. He's not about to be dinner for the undead.

"What is happening?" Danny asks, gripping his aching head in his palms. Shielding his brain away from the pretty monster.

"You're hurt—sit still," the zombie demands. He flings the fridge door open and reaches inside. "Do you need some water?" he asks, shoving a plastic bottle forward.

Then he scurries away, around the shelf, and returns, rattling a bottle of Tylenol. "Take some," he commands.

Danny accepts the water and pills, but glares suspiciously at the strange ghoul.

He gnaws his lower lip, with thick buttery brows caved in concern, and sits back on his heels. Pleased. His head tilts to the side.

This must be the most delightful zombie ever. Danny thinks.

The ghoul's mouth stretches into a half-grin.

Danny's pain subsides, as if it never existed. He moves to pull himself up off the floor.

The ghoul rushes to his feet and grips Danny's arm, offering help.

Danny gazes up at the stranger's andalusite eyes and melts for a moment. "I'm okay," he says, tugging his arm away and fixing the hem of his shirt to cover his belly. His back is soaked, and he reeks of floor cleaner.

The wet patches across the linoleum are evaporating, and the bright yellow *Caution: Wet Floor* sign is still leaning against the wall, peeking out from behind the storage room door.

"For fuck's sake, Delila," he murmurs. "She always forgets." It's not the first time he's slipped on her negligence. *Luckily, it wasn't a customer. That's a lawsuit waiting to happen.* Danny ponders that thought for a moment.

"Are you alright?" The zombie asks while leaning into Danny's peripheral.

"I'm fine," he says.

A tender kindness in the zombie's eyes gives Danny pause.

He repents, softening his tone. "I'm okay," he says.

"Oh, good." The handsome ghoul rocks on his feet. He clasps his arms behind his back and pushes his bare belly forward. A sparse trail of golden hairs trickles down his navel and disappears into the waistband of white underwear peeking out of his jeans.

Danny swallows the thick lump gathering in his throat.

"I saw you go down," the zombie says. "I was across the street." He twists around and points out the storefront window. His broad shoulders flex inside his frayed sleeves.

Danny pulls down the hem of his shirt to make sure it covers his midriff. He averts his eyes to the drink cooler, with flushed cheeks, when the zombie turns back to face him.

"Are you sure you're okay?" The zombie steps forward.

"Yes," Danny says shortly. "I'm fine." He scoots behind the shelves, kicks the mop bucket, and treks across the store. "Thanks for checking on me," Danny adds. Hinting with his tone that the stranger is welcome to go now.

The zombie rounds the front of the store and meets Danny at the counter, without breaking his watchful stare.

Danny slinks behind the register, trying to hide away from this shameful fiasco.

"That was an intense fall," the zombie comments. He leans on his elbows.

Danny grumbles, but stares at the flex of the ghoul's biceps—folded under his torso—and the long arc of his neck. His bright eyes glimmer under the fluorescents as he looks Danny up and down.

"I'm Si," he offers his hand.

Danny ignores the greeting and crouches behind the counter, pretending to engross himself in a work task. He fumbles with the box of candy bars Delilah left for him to put away.

Si stretches further over the counter and peers down at Danny.

"Danny," he finally responds, turning toward the empty shelf in aisle two, assessing the *urgent* task that's waiting. "Well, duty calls," Danny hints. Desperate to be left alone to wallow in his shame.

Si's eyes follow as Danny makes his way down the aisle. The handsome zombie dangles from his elbows off the counter, kicking his feet, before hopping back. His sneakers squeak as he bounces up behind Danny.

Oh, it's going to be a long night. Danny grumbles.

5

11:37 PM

"CAN I HELP?" SI asks, reaching out for the box of candy bars. "You probably should take it easy."

"I'm okay," Danny says, and recoils. "You don't have to stick around," he adds. "I've got tons of work to do—thanks for checking in on me."

"Danny—you just took a serious digger," Si says, shrugging and dropping his weight onto one hip. "You were out cold for quite a while."

Danny pauses, staring at the gap in the shelf, but huffs with surrender, and props his foot up on the shelves, resting the box down on his thigh, while allowing Si to support the task.

They both grab handfuls of wrapped bars, and shove them onto the shelf.

Danny peers out of the side of his eye, puzzlingly.

The clerk's T-shirt is worn and faded. His bulky body stretches the thin fabric as he moves. The blush lingering on his button nose and big ears settles back down to match his pale skin. Tiny punctures in his lobes hint at the traces of old piercings he's let go of.

His wavy dark mullet is tangled and greasy, and his body heat carries the scent of cinnamon-sugar toast. His black jeans—faded to gray—are as snug as his shirt, hugging the curves of his thighs.

Si pushes his bottom lip out and blows upward to cool his own forehead.

Danny's warm brown eyes meet his.

Si offers a smile, but Danny shies away. Yet, a hint of a grin forms at the edge of his mouth.

Finished loading the shelf, Danny scoops up the empty box.

Their fingers spark with static that tingles down through to Si's toes.

He clears his throat. "What's next?" Si asks. He's excited to *play* shopkeeper.

"Not much, honestly," Danny admits. He waddles back behind the counter.

"Are you working by yourself all night?" Si asks, concerned.

"Yeah," Danny responds hesitantly. He tears open the box bottom and flattens it against his belly. Then tucks it away in the back office.

Si leans over the counter and drags his finger over a display of lighters. Tapping the top of each one. "That must make for a long night?" Si says. Pretending to read the back of an unscratched lottery ticket, while spying up through his lashes.

Danny scopes the store, looking for his next task.

"Maybe you should sit down for a bit?" Si suggests, worried. He nods at a folded-up stool leaning against the wall behind the counter.

"I'm okay—I promise," Danny says, shrugging dismissively. But he unfurls the stool and plops down on it.

"How long have you worked here?" Si asks. He twists a crunchy curl around his finger and tugs it down, breaking the gel cast.

"Too long," Danny says. He wrinkles his face with distaste while avoiding eye contact.

Si pushes back off the counter, spins on his heels, and traipses down an aisle to browse the selection of goods.

All the typical convenience store stock. Snacks, cleaning products, air fresheners, a self-serve coffee station, an empty plexiglass box with a heat lamp to warm the hotdogs—which should be rotating inside—and two walls of refrigerators that wrap the perimeter of the store.

Si collects an energy drink and struts back to the front, drops it on the counter, and reaches for his wallet. His cheeks flare when he realizes it must be back home, with his phone. "Shit," he squeaks. "Nevermind,'" he says, and moves to return the drink.

"Take it," Danny calls out.

"I don't have my money," Si retorts, spinning back.

Danny folds bulky arms across his chest. "It's on me," he says. A sly grin slips across his face, forming a single dimple in his cheek.

Si swoons. "I can pay you later. Give me your number and I'll Apple Pay you." He snickers at his own slick flirtation.

"Don't worry about it," Danny says. He lifts off the stool and meanders toward the coffee pots. He scoops one off the ledge and heads for the back of the store.

Si pops open the energy drink and takes a long swig, setting back on the counter, before following Danny to the sink.

Danny folds over to set the thermos on the floor, and his shirt rides up his back, exposing milky skin, peppered with a dark patch of hair that swirls into the crack of his ass cleavage.

Si licks the sweet caffeinated potion off his lips and swallows the pool under his tongue.

Danny cranks the faucet and reaches for the thermos.

Si beats him to it, hauling the silver cylinder up and into the basin, pushing Danny aside with his hip.

The static between their bodies tingles as Danny stays close, watching Si fill the jug.

He peers coyly over his shoulder, and smiles.

6

11:59 PM

DANNY

WHO IS THIS GUY? Danny wonders. He studies the sweet, goldilocks'd zombie.

Si hums and shimmies, bouncing on one hip and rapping his toes, while water gushes into the thermos. He glances back over his shoulder and flashes a handsome grin while fluttering his eyelashes.

"Good?" he asks, nodding toward the coffeepot, waiting for direction to move on to the next step.

Danny nods back in agreement. His eyes are stuck on the bee-bopping ghoul.

Si twists the faucet off and hauls the full thermos out of the sink, then swishes and sways his hips as he waddles back to the coffee station.

Danny is hypnotized, but grunts to clear the pesky lump from his throat.

Si struggles to lift the heavy thermos back up onto its perch.

Danny scoops in to assist. His arm brushes against Si's naked belly, and a rush of fire blazes through him. Danny's face lights up like an ember. He quickly jerks away and shuffles back behind his counter.

"What's next?" Si asks. He floats after Danny and drapes himself across the countertop, dangling his legs, and beaming with excitement.

"That's it," Danny says with a shrug. "We're done now." *You should get going,* he bids. "I just wait for my shift to end."

A sudden faintness falls over him. He squints to steady the spinning room and sits down on the stool. Holding himself together with a quirky smile.

Si's eyes grow big with concern, and his lips pout. "Should we take you to the hospital?"

"No," Danny barks and chuckles. "I don't have insurance," he stares. "I'm fine."

"Isn't there a clinic just a few streets over?" Si asks as he steps around the counter and gently squeezes Danny's shoulder.

Static rushes through Danny's body. He ignites with electricity, and his heartbeat revs up. Sweat condenses between his shoulder blades.

"I promise—I'm good," he shorts, rising from the stool, and stepping a safe distance away from Si.

Danny slips over to the coffee station, scoops dark roast grounds into the brewer, and pours the thermos of water into the reserve. Then flicks the machine on.

Si watches over Danny, with arms folded over his bare belly, propped against the counter. He crosses one ankle over the other and juts a hip forward. Chewing his lip and raising a sculpted brow, he stares narrowly at Danny.

"Did you go to Hudson Academy?" Si asks.

"No," Danny answers, blurting out a chuckle. "I went to public school."

"Have we met before?" Si asks, tapping a finger to his lip.

Danny stares at him for a moment, blankly. Distracted by the single digit pointing out what soft pink lips the zombie has.

Si spins and leans down on his elbows. Arching his back, causing his crop-top to rise, offering a peek at his ribs.

The coffeepot gurgles and spits before settling into a steady drip. Stirring Danny out of his trance.

"You've probably been in here before." Danny assumes, but he's sure he'd remember. "Do you have a party to get to?"

Si pauses his study of the butterscotch candy package and turns to Danny with a confused expression.

Danny nods at Si's outfit. "You're all dressed up for the occasion," he states.

"Oh! Yeah," Si exclaims and giggles. "I forgot." He looks down at his ragged clothes, and then into the sliver of a mirror flanking the side of a sunglasses display. His neck flushed pink beneath the grey face paint.

Danny rolls his shoulders and grins as he spigots himself a fresh cup of coffee.

"I left the party, actually." Si spins back to the counter and leans on his elbows again.

Danny perches on his stool.

"It's my birthday, actually," Si confesses quietly. His face drops, and the gleam in his andalusite eyes dims. His elbow bumps nervously against the energy drink he'd forgotten about, but he takes a sip.

"Happy birthday," Danny cheers. Suddenly feeling responsible for Si's current emotional state. He resists the urge to offer a hug.

"Thanks," Si responds. His eyes spark up again. He tilts his head, and says, "You're actually the first person to say that today."

Danny suppresses a powerful urge to offer a hug. "Sorry," he mumbles.

Si shrugs the sadness off. "When's your birthday?" He shifts the conversation and leans further over the counter, wagging his eyebrows.

Danny stares at his mouth. Lips like candy, which probably taste as sweet. He sips his coffee.

Si fixates on Danny with his hazel eyes, flecked with gold and resembling cut gems.

"July 5th," Danny answers.

Si's pupils dilate. "You're a holiday baby too!" he chimes, and adds, "Almost."

"I guess," Danny says, chuckling. "My mother used to tell me the fireworks on the 4th were for me." His throat catches a lump again. He hadn't thought about that memory for years.

"That's so sweet," Si says, beaming.

His eyes gloss over.

Is he going to cry? Danny worries.

"My parents have never remembered mine," Si says. "No one does." He spins away and studies a candy display. "Halloween takes center stage."

The wisps of curls, clung to Si's neck, capture Danny's stare.

"Our nanny was the only one who remembered," Si says. He props a pair of sunglasses onto his nose and checks his reflection. "Is there a bathroom I can use?"

Danny nods. "Sure," he says, pointing toward the door at the back of the store, which leads to the basement storage space, and rest room. "The bathroom is at the bottom of the stairs."

Si smiles. "I'll be right back," he announces, and trots toward the door.

"Be careful," Danny cautions. He tracks blond curls as they bounce over the long shelf of chips, headed toward the back of the store. "The nanny?" he murmurs under his breath, and chuffs.

7

12:13 PM

Si

THE RICKETY WOODEN STAIRS creak and moan as Si descends into the basement. Concrete walls narrow into the dark dungeon. A cold waft triggers goosebumps up his arms, and the reek of mildew tickles his nostrils.

Si tugs on a string dangling from a rafter—tickling his ear—and the light flickers on. Piles of boxes and clutter, draped in cobwebs, fill the damp storage space.

He pokes his head into the toilet closet while his fingers search the wall for a light switch. With a flick, an old dressing-room style mirror, trimmed in bulbs, and hung above a sink basin, turns on.

Si closes himself in the little room and twists the faucet on. He studies his ghoulish face in the mirror, scoffing at his own sloppy makeup skills, and begins scrubbing it away. The gray water circles the drain and disappears, gurgling.

He peeks out the door, immediately spots a box of paper towel rolls, and shuffles out to collect one. A hanging-rack of clothes, tucked into a far corner, catches his eye.

"Well, that's convenient," Si says. He peers down at his tattered crop-top and chuffs, then wades through a clutter of stacked boxes and chooses a purple button-down—slightly large, but sufficient.

He slips back into the toilet, rearranges his curls and dries his face. Then peels off the costume crop-too and twirls into the purple shirt. It sags on his lanky frame, but he rolls the sleeves up to his elbows and leaves his old top in a pile atop a box.

With a tug, the light flicks off, and the basement goes dark again. He races up the stairs, toward the fluorescent sanctuary at the top, to escape the things in the dark that might follow him.

Danny continues to perch on his stool, sip his coffee, and gaze out the window at the quiet street. His pale cheeks softly flushed with peachy hues, and the artery in his thick neck pulsed under his skin.

He turns toward Si as he rounds the shelves and crosses the store, heading back to the counter, offering a slow spin along the way.

One dimple forms at the edge of Danny's half-smile. His gleaming eyes scan Si from head to toe and back, lingering on his chest for a moment.

Si puffs up to give him a brief show.

8

12:29 PM

DANNY

"Where'd you find the shirt?" Danny asks. His eyes gleam as he studies the garment, then move up to meet Si's, where they both linger in a quiet gaze.

Si winks and draws a long swig from his energy drink. "Much better—right?" he says, flashing a wide, toothy smile.

Danny's dimple pokes deeper.

The billowing purple fabric drapes over Si's subtly sun-toasted skin, contrasting his buttery curls with their fresh tidiness and luminescent sheen. Undoubtedly on purpose, he unbuttoned the top three buttons, offering a tempting new view, in exchange for covering up his belly.

Danny licks the bitter coffee taste from his lips. Suddenly, craving something sweet.

"So what do you do while you're waiting for your shift to end?" Si asks. His chest cleaves as he crosses his arms and leans his elbows down onto the counter.

"This is it," Danny says. Winging his arms out and swinging side to side. His eyes drop a bit as he scans the store, reminded of his mundane existence.

Si offers an intoxicating smile. His crystalline eyes beam, even when he squints.

Danny can't resist absorbing a bit of Si's sunny aura. His gravity is magnetic.

"I don't believe I've ever been here before," Si announces. Returning to their previous conversation. "We must know each other from somewhere else?" he adds. Chewing his lip and rocking on his elbows, he studies Danny intently, searching for the answer.

Danny shrugs and stares back at the golden-haired beauty. "Are you sure?" he asks.

Si's familiarity is baffling.

Danny isn't sure if he'd ever forget encountering such a shiny being. His sharp mind is typically great at recording memories, and linking faces with even the briefest moment

in time. *Maybe I'm still shattered from the fall?* He wonders.

"You may have come in, and just don't remember?"
Danny suggests.

Si stares at Danny's face, puckers his candy-pink lips,
and rolls his shoulders in surrender.

Danny flushes, but looks out over the store. He spots
an askew shelf of crackers and deserts his position to make
adjustments.

Si remains draped over the counter as Danny turns back.

The revived angel is arching his back—displaying a per-
fectly round ass—and peering over his shoulder from the
corner of his eye.

Danny sucks back a pearl of drool trying to escape the
edge of his grin. *If he doesn't leave here soon, I'm going to
devour him,* he thinks. Suddenly starving.

"Wait—do you know Trent Wagner?" Si asks. "Were
you at Chad's wedding?" He rises onto his palms, arching
his back deeper.

Danny releases a heated sigh and bites the inside of his
cheek. "No," he says, shaking his head.

Si flips over and leans back on his elbows. His shirt
stretches wide open across his chest, and his belly peeks out
between the fastened buttons.

Tease, Danny accuses—in his mind. "I have no idea who that is," he says, and turns away to adjust a shelf of snack cakes.

"Hmmm?" Si queries as he maunders laps around a gift card display. He drags his fingers across the glossy cards, which clap and swoon under his touch.

Danny envies those lucky cards at that moment. He tugs down the hem of his t-shirt and adjusts the front of his jeans. Twisting away to go fill a fresh cup of coffee. Needing to quench his thirst.

"Would you like a cup?" he offers Si. "Or should you get going?"

"It's so quiet. Don't you listen to music while you're working?" Si says, redirecting the conversation. He plants his feet in a wide stance—clenching perfect ass cheeks—and pushes his belly forward on his hips. He studies a random gift card with furrowed brows and puckered lips.

The room spins for a second, and Danny leans against the coffee bar ledge to steady himself.

"I do, usually," he responds. "Delila—on second shift—likes to work in silence." He struts into the back office and flips the stereo on. Peeking his head back out to the store, he asks, "Any requests?" *Why do I keep inviting him to stay?* He ponders and waits.

"What do you usually listen to?" Si asks and smiles squinty.

"Good question," Danny answers. He turns the dial and searches for a familiar tune.

A raucous voice bellows wildly inappropriate lyrics about *fucking like animals*, but Danny quickly fumbles the dial further on. He settles on a yacht-rock ballad from decades past. It serenades from the ceiling speakers.

"Oh, I love this song," Si calls back

"Of course you do," Danny says under his breath with a soft chuckle.

Xylophone keys chime over a smooth rhythmic beat, counting notes, and a saxophone wails the sweet melody. A whining singer begs to sail away, to where they've always heard it could be free.

Danny returns to the floor, where Si is swaying raptly with the music. Dancing down the aisle with long slow strides.

Danny takes a seat on his stool, sips his coffee, and settles down for the show.

"This reminds me of Nanny Grace," Si says, reminiscing. He looks thoughtful, his face dreamy. "She used to listen to this sort of music while cleaning up, or cooking for us." He twirls down the center aisle, rolling his head and closing his eyes, mouthing the lyrics.

Danny turns to gaze out the window, but stares at the Si show, broadcasting in the dark reflection. His body movements are mesmerizing, and his free spirit is luminous.

Si bops and shimmies to the back of the store.

"Do you still see her?" Danny asks.

Si turns back, with sadness in his expression. He steps up to the chip shelf and crinkles a bag.

"No—she died when I was thirteen," he responds. Swiping his cheek with the back of his hand. Fluorescent light glimmers off his curls.

"Sorry," Danny says.

"It was a long time ago," Si replies and shrugs. "She was like a mother though." He trots back to the counter.

"I lost my mother ten years ago," Danny sympathizes, unsure why.

"Sorry," Si says, frowning. He leans down on folded arms, cleaving his chest.

"Thanks," Danny responds, sipping his coffee to quench his thirst. He gulps.

"What about your father?" Si asks.

"Never knew him," Danny replies bluntly.

"Me neither—really," Si says. He folds his wrist and dangles the energy drink in his fingers, swirling the fizzing can. "My parents both traveled a lot." His eyes travel down to Danny's t-shirt.

Danny shifts with discomfort. Wishing he'd worn something nicer. "I'm sorry you lost your parents," he consoles.

"Oh no. My parents are alive," Si says and chuckles. "They're sitting on a yacht, somewhere off the coast of Santorini—I think?" He gazes up at the security camera, looking for an answer.

"A yacht?" Danny scoffs.

Si flushes red.

Danny sips coffee to shut himself up.

"Yeah," Si spins and floats away to the dairy cooler.

"You really don't need to hang around this place. It's going to get boring real soon," Danny announces.

"I don't have anywhere to be." Si folds over with his nose inches from the glass door, studying rows of milk.

9

1:42 AM

Sensing he's being pushed toward the exit, he stares past the blackened windows, at a murky stillness in the street. Curious. Si looks back at Danny, who seems drowsy, and worries that the clerk is still suffering from his fall.

"Is it always this quiet?" Si asks, nodding toward the outside. "Halloween isn't over yet—where is everybody?"

"It's past midnight." Danny replies.

"But the sun hasn't come up yet," Si quips. His attention drifts back to the refrigerator. "Hmm ... Coffee milk, is that good?" he asks, turning to face the clerk.

Danny's eyes race away from Si's backside. The edge of his grin peeks over the side of his face, but his blushing reflection in the glass storefront is validation.

Si offers a little shimmy, but it goes unnoticed.

Danny isn't Si's usual type. At least, not like anyone he's ever gravitated toward before. He doesn't look like any boy or man he's dated before. They're usually taller, athletic, academic, and completely vapid.

Danny is shorter, and stout. He's mysterious, but magnetic and intriguing. Rough edges match his tattered jeans and taut faded tee. But the way he turns the toes of his chunky unlaced combat boots inward gives his tenderness away.

Si spins on his heels, curls his shoulders in, and stuffs his hands in his pockets, meandering back toward the counter.

The entry bell chimes as the door swings open.

A young couple—who materialize from the dark void outside—carry in a chilly wind, which pulls the door closed as it enters. They squeeze past Si and march straight to the back of the store.

Danny's eyes narrow and his energy shifts as he tracks their movement.

Si pauses behind the gift card display and keeps watch over the scene. "Do we know them?" He whispers.

Danny doesn't hear him. His intense stare doesn't waver.

Si steps up to the counter and taps Danny's arm. Static sparks between the touch, startling Danny's focus back to him.

He rubs the charged area on his arm, creasing his brows, with saucer-wide pupils boring into Si.

"Fruitbat?" the young man calls out.

He's lanky, dressed in a vintage *Cranberries: World Tour* t-shirt and ripped skinny jeans, painted on spindly legs. Checkered Chucks slap against the floor, and goopy mascara clings to his eyelashes.

Danny cringes and freezes. Terrified, maybe. His hands grip the edge of the counter, flexing his thick biceps.

"How the hell are you?" the guy carries on. "Ames, you remember Fruitbat, don't you?" He sets a carrier of beer on the counter and turns to the petite brunette.

She's dressed in a black camisole, over a little white t-shirt, and a black leather jacket, adorned with silver grommets, matching a leather miniskirt with chunky boots.

As a kid, they're the sort that used to intrigue Si fearfully. *Very retro-goth. They must be coming from a Halloween party too,* he assumes.

Si shimmies to the side of Danny's counter, hiding between magazine and gum displays, while the clerk acquaints himself with old friends.

10

2:10 AM

DANNY

AMES NODS AND SAYS. "Hey Danny." She's soft-spoken, and her sweet face hasn't aged a bit since they all attended high school together.

The couple had made headlines after crashing Grayden's motorcycle into a tree the night they all graduated. They seem well now.

"Hey," Danny groans, dragging the six-pack of beer toward himself. The clink of bottles echoes in the thickly tense space between him and the visitors.

"What have you been up to, man?" Grayden asks. He still reeks of arrogance. Like it's some stinky designer fragrance.

Danny avoids eye contact. His nose wrinkles, and his bittersweet grin reads more like a disconcerting sneer. "You two are still together?" he remarks. Holding his stare on the cash register.

Grayden Sloan and Amy Kilpatrick were codependent monarchs of their gothic clique. *It's no surprise they're still attached to each other,* Danny posits. Although he always thought Ames could do better than Grayden.

The cash register beeps when Danny scans their purchase.

"Twelve seventy-eight," he reports.

"Man, things are expensive now." Grayden slaps a bill on the counter. "Hey, are you still writing?"

Danny is taken aback by the question. Grayden used to tease him about his *hobby.*

"Yep," Danny shorts and braces for a snide remark.

Grayden once snatched Danny's journal out of his hands, and read an entry aloud, in front of their entire social circle. It just happened to be a confession of his lustful fantasy involving their friend Bobby—outing Danny to everyone.

He was mortified, and at that moment they nicknamed him "Fruitbat."

"Good," Grayden says, smiling. "You're great at it, you know?"

Danny's eyes finally lift from the cash register, and he stares directly at Grayden. "Do you want a bag?" he asks.

"No," Grayden says, and chuckles. "It was great seeing you."

Danny is stunned and doesn't respond.

"Later, Fruitbat," Grayden says, collecting his beer and Ame's hand. He leads her toward the door.

Danny's face singes.

"See ya around, Danny," Amy says with a warm smile.

The pair slip through the door and disappear into the night.

Danny pushes the register closed. It dings in unison with the slam and jingle of the door.

"They seem nice." Si says. He floats back around the counter and leans on one hand.

"That guy was such an asshole," Danny grumbles, then adds, "Amy was okay."

"Why'd he call you Fruitbat?" Si queries.

"I was the queer goth kid of our friend group back in high school," Danny replies.

Si leans down on his elbow and hooks his thumb in a belt loop of his jeans. His shirt slips down off his shoulder, exposing more of his chest.

Danny clears his throat, staring.

"It's a cute name," Si cheers.

"Ironically, it's a slur. He might as well just call me a *faggot,*" Danny snarks and adds. "It also means *loser.*"

"Oh," Si says, stunned. "That's …"

"I didn't know at first," Danny interrupts. "Honestly, I'm not sure Grayden knows what he's saying. He's not the brightest." He chuckles.

Si shrugs. "Own it—it's still cute," he says, grinning. "We are *faggots* after all." He winks and twirls on his foot, then traipses to the coffee bar. "And you're not a loser."

Danny smiles, with a twinkle in his eye.

11

2:27 AM

"YOU SHOULD SMILE MORE," Si suggests. "It's beautiful."
He beams with a wide smile and squinted eyes. "So, you're
a writer?" he asks as he taps the tops of the thermoses.

"I dabble," Danny mutters shyly.

Si trots back to the counter. "What do you write?" he
asks, gazing down at the gum display along the counter
front. He drags his finger across the wrappers.

"Garbage," Danny snorts. "According to publishers."

"I doubt that," Si says matter-of-factly. "Wait, the papers
in your bag? Is that your writing?" His face flushes red, realizing his confession to noseying through Danny's things.

Danny quirks a brow and stares confusedly.

"I was looking for a phone earlier—when you were passed out," Si says. "Sorry." He swigs from the lukewarm energy drink and sneers at the can.

"Oh ..." Danny blurts.

Si flashes a wide grin, inviting Danny to follow suit.

"I bet it's amazing—I have a friend in publishing. Her taste is horrendous. Don't tell *her* I said so," Si proclaims. He stares at Danny, waiting for a response.

The edge of Danny's mouth curls up, and his dimple pokes in.

"Could I read some?" Si asks. He drapes himself over the counter, kicks his feet up behind him, and flutters his eyelids. His face is close enough to capture a whiff of Danny's cinnamon-toast scent, tinged with a hint of coffee breath.

"Sure," Danny responds with uncertainty.

—But he doesn't move to collect the bundle of papers.

Si jumps back off the counter and wags a finger toward the office, asking for permission with raised brows.

Danny nods, averting his eyes out the window.

Si shuffles back to the desk and pulls the folder out of Danny's bag. He returns to the counter and lays the manuscript out before himself.

Danny squirms off the stool, monitoring Si, while he wanders away from the counter.

"Are you sure this is okay?" Si asks before he digs in to Danny's work.

Danny nods. "Go ahead," he says, but adds with a rush, "It still needs more edits."

Si hugs the precious treasure to his chest and strolls to the back of the store. He sits down cross-legged on the floor in the far corner, beneath the "wine" section of shelves, and spreads the folder open on his lap.

"It's kinda dark ..." Danny warns.

Si smiles back at him and digs in.

12

2:48 AM

DANNY

DANNY SLINKS DOWN AN aisle, nervously adjusting products, while he keeps Si in his peripheral. He returns to the front and rounds the gift card rack, dragging his fingers along the same cards Si had touched. Lingering static tingles on his skin.

He stretches his neck to peer down the aisle, checking Si is still there.

Si is huddled over the pages, chewing his cheek and caressing his chin.

Danny stares, studying Si's expressions, trying to read his opinion.

Si's eyes lift—catching Danny—and he sucks his lip in.

Danny spins away, continuing to tidy the display, and moves to do the same with a shelf of vitamins and pain relievers. His cheeks flush pink, and he shakes away another woozy spell. With a deep inhale, he packs away the little stars flickering in his eyes.

His belly growls for sustenance.

"Are you hungry?" Danny calls back.

"Starved!" Si chimes.

"Do you like frozen pizza?" Danny asks.

"Of course!" Si responds.

Danny gathers two boxes from a freezer and lugs them into the back office. He pops the two pizzas into a vintage toaster oven and leans back to peek out the doorframe.

Si is unmoved. Folded over his lap, propping his elbows on his knees and holding his own face up in his palms. His lashes flit while his eyes scan the papers, but he's still unreadable.

The toaster oven ticks rhythmically, like a time-bomb.

Danny shuffles out to the floor and fumbles to organize an end-cap of candy-flavored lip glosses. He pops several of their caps open to test the scents—trying to determine which one might taste like Si's sweet lips—until the store floods with the aroma of baking dough, herb sauce, and toasted cheese.

The toaster oven *dings* an alert, announcing its finished working.

Danny struts back to the office, grabbing a quick side-glance of Si. He peels two sheets off a paper towel roll for makeshift plates.

When he turns back, about to call out …

Si is standing in the doorway. Beaming. "Your writing is so good!" he cheers.

Danny studies his wide eyes and giddy smile. He's sincere. The piping hot pizzas are burning his fingertips. "Ouch!" he blurts and quickly sets both steaming discs on the desk.

Si chuckles. "Are you okay?" he reaches out and cups Danny's hands in his own, leaning in to blow on and soothe his pain.

Danny doesn't recoil—as he usually would—but marvels at the handsome angel. "You really think it's good?" Danny asks in a low and blank tone.

"I'm no critic," Si starts, but meets Danny's eyes with a pause. "But honestly, I love it." He finishes with a warm smile and a gleam in his eyes.

"That's nice of you," Danny says, and slowly pulls his hands back. "Eat up." He nods toward their dinners.

Si carefully scoops up one pizza and perches one butt cheek on the edge of the desk, dangling his leg. "Danny, I'm serious. It's great—you're magnificent."

Danny sits on the folding chair—blushing—and folds his pizza in half before he takes a big bite. "Thank you," he says.

"Why don't you self-publish?" Si asks, he folds his pizza and takes a big bite. Slurping up the sauce and cheese that squeeze out onto his chin.

Danny chuffs. "I don't know—I've thought about it," he says with a shrug. "I think it's expensive."

Si stares into his pizza for a moment, and then says, "What about an investor?"

Danny snorts and says, "I wouldn't know where to find one."

Si lights up and taps Danny's shoulder with a static finger. "You just did," he says.

Danny stares at a cluttered corkboard on the wall as his brows cave in on his softening forehead.

"I'll invest in your book—you don't need a publisher." Si says.

"You don't even know me," Danny says.

Si silently gazes down upon Danny with a sage grin. He sparkles in a fluorescent aura.

"That's kind, but I can't take your money," Danny responds.

"It's not even mine, really," Si says. "My father has plenty to go around." He chuckles.

Si's grin might be sinister if he weren't so handsome.

He takes another big bite and squints while he chews.

"Wanna get out of here and go for a walk?" Danny asks. "I could use some air."

"Sure!" Si blurts without hesitation. "I'd love to." He beams excitedly. "Will you get in trouble?" he asks, chewing on his last bite and crumpling the warm paper towel in his hands.

Danny stands up, gathers Si's trash with his own, and drops the balled-up papers into the trash. He gathers a hooded sweatshirt draped on the back of the chair and ties it around his waist. Then, he slips his bag over his head and settles the strap across his chest. "Let's go," he says, jingling a ring of keys in his hand.

Si hops off the desk, and squeezes ahead of Danny. He jogs to the front door, which jingles as he holds it open.

"They won't even notice I'm gone," Danny says, as he ushers Si through the door ahead of himself. He locks up behind them.

"Where should we go?" Si asks, teetering on his heels.

"I'm not sure," Danny says. "We'll just see where the wind takes us."

Si folds his arms and shivers.

"Here," Danny says. He pulls the sweatshirt from his waist and holds it out to Si.

"I'm okay," Si responds.

"Take it," Danny insists. "I don't really need it—I run hot."

Si giggles and reaches out to accept the offer. His static fingers shock Danny's thumb, and it lifts the hairs up his arm.

The autumn air is sharp, with just a hint of humidity, as rolling temperatures collide, creating a slight fog hanging over the tops of the buildings and a breeze scrapes crinkled paper wrappers across the pavement. The city smells sweet and nutty, like someone is baking peanut butter cookies.

"The park?" Si suggests.

"Sure," Danny's eyes sparkle in the fluorescent light spilling out of the window.

They start up the sidewalk.

13

3:13 AM

"THE STREETS ARE SO quiet, aren't they?" Si notes, scanning the street skeptically, as if he's waiting for something to jump out at them. He double-knots the sleeves hugging his belly.

"It's late—or early," Danny replies. "Don't worry, you're safer than you think." His head tilts downward, focusing on the ground ahead of their steps.

Si gently nudges Danny's shoulder with his own and stares down at the clerk's hand, swinging with his stride, breezing past Si's pinky—tempting him to grab ahold. Si inhales the sweet cinnamon toast wafting on the chilly air.

Danny stuffs his hands in his pockets, as if he senses Si's trepidation and pushes away the opportunity. "You really like my story?" he asks again.

Si pauses on his feet and says, "I'd love to read more."

"I need to write more," Danny scoffs.

"What's stopping you?" Si says, restarting his feet and scurrying to close the gap between them.

"Honestly ... It's been years." Danny mutters.

"How come?" Si queries.

Danny rolls his shoulders up and turns away, gazing across the street. "I think I shut down for a bit," he says.

"Years—is longer than *a bit*," Si responds. He stares at the side of Danny's face and studies the warm glow of streetlights painting his cheek and sharp points in his messy hair.

Danny's body shivers.

"Do you need your sweatshirt?" Si asks.

"No, I run hot," Danny lies.

Si snickers and says, "Okay."

Red and blue lights flash up, around the bend, painting the side of brick buildings with violet hues. The surface of the river is glimmering like sequins and reflecting a scene across the bridge. Three police cruisers are parked in a row, and the drivers are investigating something.

Danny and Si pause at the corner of the sidewalk. The tiptoes of Si's sneakers hung over the concrete ledge. He wraps his arms around himself and rubs his skin for warmth, then slips the sweatshirt off his waist and pulls it on. "That intersection is so dangerous," he says. He turns to Danny. "I nearly had a truck take me out." He points and adds, "Right there."

Danny gnaws his cheek and says, "Let's go this way."

Si zips up the hoodie—its spicy scent is divine—and follows Danny into the turn. He peeks back across the river.

A rescue wagon joins the cruisers, and two EMTs rush out to join the officers, taking a statement from a slender man in running gear, who must have witnessed the accident.

"That's not good," Danny says, peering back and nodding, as the EMTs cart a dark plastic bag, atop their stretcher, into the rig. "C'mon," he says, motioning to Si.

Si skips forward and catches up. "The mayor needs to do something about that," he says. *I'll get my mother on the case,* he chuckles.

They follow along, parallel to the river.

Si recognizes a small tattoo studio, where he had accompanied Mallory for her first, and only piece. The dainty daisy illustration on her shoulder flashes in his mind. The shop looks abandoned, but it might just be closed for the evening.

"Why are your creative juices blocked?" he asks, returning to their previous conversation. Si shoves his hands in the hoodie pockets and fiddles with a lint ball.

"I shut down after my mother died," Danny confesses. "She used to keep me going, even when publishers turned me down." He stares at the ground.

"I'm sorry," Si whispers.

"It was a decade ago now—I still jot down ideas, I just haven't drafted them out since her funeral." Danny says.

"What happened to her?" Si asks, adding, "You don't have to talk about it if you don't want to, of course."

"Cancer," Danny responds.

"Oh, yeah … Nancy Grace too," Si starts. "I never got to see her after she got sick—and couldn't work for us any longer."

"Oh, man. I'm really sorry," Danny says softly. He drops his hands out of his pockets again. His arm swings with his stride.

Si reaches over and grabs his wrist. He slips his hand down and weaves their fingers together.

Danny's eyes spark wide, and his face flushes pink. He tenses up.

Si smiles and squeezes his hand. "Relax," he whispers soothingly.

Danny softens, and they carry on.

Si lets out a long exhale and stares ahead.

"You said you left a party tonight?" Danny says, cutting the silence.

"My friends never miss a chance to host a gathering." Si says sarcastically.

"But they forgot it's your birthday?" Danny asks, grimacing.

"Grace would have reminded them," Si says.

"I think you need better friends," Danny states.

"I think I've found one," Si responds and giggles.

Danny's fingers wiggle and stroke Si's knuckles. The shy clerk licks a dried bite of pizza sauce from the corner of his mouth as his eyes reflect the sequined shimmer off the river.

14

3:33 AM

DANNY

DANNY IS TAKEN ABACK by the peculiar sensation. His arm is buzzing with static. The vibrations hum tenderly throughout his entire body. *Why am I just now meeting you?* He wonders.

Si sparkles beneath the streetlights. His aura is iridescent. As if the full spectrum of the rainbow emanates from him.

Danny has seen nothing like this before.

"Someone is doing some baking.," he states, observing the peanut butter cookie scented air. "It smells delicious."

He smiles, delighted. "The city usually reeks of fish because of the river," he adds.

"I noticed that earlier," Si responds. He wiggles his fingers and squeezes a fresh batch of static up Danny's arm. "There must be a bakery nearby? They must be setting up for the day ahead."

"My mother used to make amazing peanut butter cookies. The sort you press a fork into and make that cross-hatched pattern," Danny says and demonstrates the technique with his free hand. "She used to let me do that part." He inhales deeply to savor the tasty air.

"Mmm, I used to love hanging out in the kitchen with Grace," Si relates. "She'd dance with me while dinner cooked."

"That must be where you get those moves from?" Danny says, giggling and then blushing shyly.

Si slows to a stop. He tugs back on Danny's arm.

Danny turns around to face him.

Si's hazel eyes are glimmering and wanton. He sucks in air, saying, "Will you kiss me?"

Danny gawks at him, stunned.

Si's face drops, disheartened. "Sorry, I know that was weird," he murmurs.

Danny steps forward—seizing the moment before it passes—their faces are just inches apart, exchanging chilly clouds of breath, back and forth. He raises his chin and leans up for their lips to touch. The static in his body sizzles and pops like sparklers set off.

Sticky lips peel apart as Danny steps backward, dumbfounded and intoxicated. "Happy birthday," he whispers shakily.

Si wraps his arms around Danny's neck and smashes their faces together again.

He stumbles back against the brick facade of an art gallery, pulling Danny with him.

Weak in the knees, relying on the building for upright support. They kiss.

Si whimpers softly into Danny's mouth. He is even sweeter than he'd imagined like this would be.

Si's fingers tangle in tufts of Danny's hair on the back of his neck, sending shockwaves trickling down his spine.

Danny reaches around Si, fumbly slipping his hands up underneath his shirt, and caresses the velvety plain of his bare back.

Heavy breaths flare from their nostrils, and goosebumps sow their skin.

Si pauses the kiss, keeping their lips pressed together, and asks, "Is your place nearby?" His tone is low and hungry.

"Around the corner," Danny replies.

"Take me there," Si demands.

His hands bracket Danny's cheeks. He pecks his lips again and then pushes Danny forward.

Danny clasps Si's hand and leads him down the sidewalk, around the bend, and onto the stoop of a raggedy old Victorian house turned apartment building.

The door squawks open, and peanut butter cookie air follows them inside. It whirls throughout the foyer and climbs the rickety three-story stairwell with them.

Danny stares ahead, eager. Until they reach the door to his place. He doesn't dare look back, for fear the dreamy zombie will have disappeared.

Still lit with static, he finally dares to look back.

Si is beaming with anticipation.

Danny pauses for a moment. His mind is scattered with thoughts. *I know he doesn't know. It's not for me to tell ... He'll figure it out.*

Danny reboots, unlocks the door, and shoves it open. The door bounces against the wall.

Danny pulls Si inside.

15

3:44 AM

Sı

THEY WHIRL INTO THE apartment and crash against the back of the door, slamming it shut.

Giggling, like boys getting up to devious things.

Danny steps further inside and flicks on a table lamp next to his bed.

The studio apartment is a single room—that could fit entirely inside Si's bedroom. A crow's nest at the edge of the building's attic. The walls slant in and meet at a single peak with just one large window offering a view of the city's rooftops and starry sky. A small kitchenette huddles in a corner, next to a claw-foot bathtub, toilet, and sink—separated by a plastic shower curtain posing as a makeshift wall.

Si steps forward. He peels off the sweatshirt, lays it at the foot of the bed, crosses his arms and rocks on his feet. "It's warm in here," he says.

Danny nods. He crawls over the bed, and cranks a latch, flipping the skylight open, just a crack. "My landlord—Ms. Cooper—lives on the first floor. She's a frail eighty-six-year-old, who grew up in the Caribbean." He chuckles and adds, "So the entire building gets to suffer her tropical nostalgia."

The cold from the window cools the air in the apartment.

Si studies Danny, and the temperate shift in his demeanor from the time they rushed lustfully up the stairs, until crossing the threshold into his space. His cheeks are flushed, and his eyes are avoidant.

"Thirsty?" Danny asks. He moves toward a mini-fridge, set atop a shelving unit that holds a small amount of dry goods and ingredients—familiar packaging to the convenience store's stocks.

"I'm good," Si answers with a slight chuckle. He turns his body and follows in one step, reaching out to grab Danny's hand, but he misses.

Danny wings his arms out and says, "This is my place." Apologetically.

"I love it," Si cheers.

A scattered collection of crystals and metaphysical trinkets catches his attention. Books are piled on top of and spill over a three-tiered case. More stacks peek out from underneath the bed, which is draped in an old handmade quilt. Tattered at its edges, just like Danny.

Si folds over to peer into a small round fishbowl, sprouting a stalk of bamboo, and hosting a bright blue-violet beta. The fish performs a spin and sprawls its waving fins.

"That's Spectra," Danny says.

"She's stunning," Si chimes.

"She's a he—I think," Danny responds.

"Oh?" Si says. He gently taps a finger against the glass and traces invisible circles, following the dancing fish.

"The males are usually vibrant colors and have more exaggerated fins," Danny adds.

Si stands upright and spins around. "Makes sense," he says with a wink.

Danny's cheeks flush, and a single dimple pokes his cheek.

Si closes the distance between them and holds his face close to Danny's. He stares down at the clerk's lips, closes his eyes, and leans in. But only kisses the air.

He opens his eyes.

Danny has reclaimed the distance, blushing. Averting his eyes.

"What's the matter?" Si asks solemnly.

"I don't really hook up with strangers," Danny says.

"Oh—me neither," Si responds. A flush of shame rises up his neck. He steps back, bumps into Spectra's bowl, and fumbles to steady the quake he's caused. Ripples settle back down, and the beta performs a pirouette.

A deck of cards tumbles out of the side table that holds up the fish tank, and they spread across the floor.

"You read tarot?" Si asks.

"My mother used to," Danny replies and adds. "She taught me how."

"Tell my fortune?" Si pleads.

Danny scoffs. He bends over and collects the cards, stacking them in his palm, and then shuffles the deck. "Have a seat," he says, jerking his head toward the bed.

Si lifts one leg up, folding it beneath him, and plops down. Lit with anticipation.

Danny perches on the edge of the bed, mirroring his guest. He draws a deep inhale into his chest and taps the deck on his knee.

16

3:59 AM

DANNY

THE CARDS FAN OUT and slip back into a neat pile, repeatedly, in Danny's hands.

"Think of a question," he requests.

Si ponders, mesmerized, staring at the magic deck.

One card leaps out of the shuffle and lands face-down on the bedspread.

Danny flips it right-side up to reveal the *Fool* card.

Si wrinkles his nose, and his eyes rise to meet Danny's, eager for an explanation.

"New beginnings," Danny responds. "You're starting off on a new adventure ..." He flips the next card, revealing the *Ace of Wands.* He lays it across the *Fool.* "You have, or will change your mind about something," he continues, and flips another card, laying it down above the crossed duo. The *Eight of Cups.* "You're leaving behind things that weren't serving you."

Si's eyes grow wide, and he chuffs.

Danny fans the cards and lays the next down. The *Six of Swords.* "You're about to journey through a portal ..." He flips the next card down—*Death.*

Si lets out a gasp.

Danny chuckles and says, "It just means a transition ... That's already happened." He points. "See how it's positioned beneath the others?"

Si relaxes and grins.

Danny flips the next four cards, lining them up alongside the Celtic cross he'd created with the first set. *The Chariot, The High Priestess,* the *Two of Cups,* and last, *Judgement.*

He inhales and says, "Your next journey is guided by a divine force, alongside a new companion, into the next phase." Danny stares down at the cards silently.

"That sounds fantastic," Si cheers.

He touches Danny's hand, and static sparks up.

Danny smiles. He reaches a hand around the back of Si's neck and pulls him forward. Pressing their lips together. A shiver runs down through his body, and he pulls back.

Si gawks at him, frozen in confusion. "What's the matter?" he asks.

Danny looks out to the moon. "It's not tomorrow yet," he murmurs mysteriously.

The celestial orb blinks behind a fluffy white cloud passing by.

He hops up off the bed, and scurries to the kitchenette.

Si slumps back on his elbow, pressing into Danny's pillows. He huffs with frustration.

Danny fumbles in the single cabinet. Plates rattle. He reaches over to his bag and clutches it to his belly, out of Si's view. A plastic wrapper crinkles, and then a flick of flint ignites a glow.

Danny spins around—beaming—holding out a plate with a single hostess cupcake and a lit candle poking up from it. "Happy birthday," he cheers.

Si melts. The candlelight reflects in his watery eyes.

"Make your wish," Danny requests.

Si inhales, and blows the tiny fire out. He stretches his neck and kisses Danny's dimpled cheek.

"Thank you," he whispers crackly, into the sweet clerk's ear.

Danny pulls the candle off the cake before the wax can drip. "Enjoy," he says.

Si takes a bite and then holds the cake up to Danny's lips.

"It's all yours," Danny says, shaking his head.

"Mm-mmm ..." Si mumbles, shaking his head with his mouth full. He swallows and insists, "Have a bite." Shoving the cake at Danny's lips.

Danny surrenders and bites, staring directly into Si's eyes while he chews.

Si beams with delight, and takes a second bite.

"The rest is yours," Danny says, refusing the last segment.

Si shrugs and pops the rest into his mouth. He hands Danny the empty plate and drops back onto the edge of the bed.

"Should I tell you what I wished for?" he teases.

"Absolutely not—it won't come true if you do," Danny responds.

Si hums and giggles. "It already has," he mumbles.

Danny blushes and hops onto the bed. Splaying out on his belly, hugging pillows against his cheek.

Si reclines back and twirls fingers in Danny's hair.

17

4:32 AM

Si spies a TV remote on the nightstand. He scoops it up and pokes a button. The wall-mounted screen blips on to static until Si scrolls.

Danny rolls onto his side and lays his head against Si's shoulder.

Shows flip by, like the shuffle of the tarot cards.

They watch a few moments of a cooking competition, then some new home-buyers touring potential abodes, and half an episode of a ghost-hunting series.

Danny's wild hair tickles Si's exposed clavicle. It faintly smells of apples, which blends with his cinnamon toast perfume deliciously.

Si stares down at the clerk while he flicks through TV stations, paying no attention to where he pauses. He pecks Danny's forehead.

"We bring you a devastating story this post-Halloween morning," the newscaster starts. His pearly white smile drops for a serious matter. He's standing on the dangerous median with the bridge, the river, and the chaotic street lights backdropping the scene. He continues, "Someone discovered the hit-and-run victim at the intersection of Tukee Bridge and Wilton Highway." Winging an arm out to direct the camera to pan over the river. His speech rolls on, off camera. "Be warned, you're about to see the victim, post mortem, in hopes someone will reach out to verify his identity."

Danny lifts on his elbow and reaches for the remote in Si's hand.

Si swings it out of Danny's grasp. He chuckles teasingly.

"Let me see it." Danny's eyes are big with panic.

Si's face shows up on the screen. Pale-gray skin—still in zombie makeup—with sunken smoky eyes, closed in peaceful slumber.

"Wait," Si blurts and bolts upright.

Danny shrinks away.

"That's me!" Si squeaks. He turns to Danny with a gaunt, confused expression.

Danny reaches for the remote again. A spark ignites as Danny touches Si's arm. The TV blips off, and static fills the entire room.

"What is happening?" Si pleads for the answer.

"You're okay," Danny whispers soothingly.

"Danny, what was that?" Si asks.

"I should have told you," Danny murmurs. He lowers his face.

"What?" Si echoes. "What is happening?"

"The scene at the bridge—" Danny starts.

"The SUV—" Si says with a pause, "It hit me?" He questions Danny, but adds, "I rolled out of the way."

"You did, but your body didn't," Danny responds.

"That doesn't make sense," Si says. He stares at the TV's darkened screen.

"The soul separates from the body when a traumatic death happens," Danny explains.

"I'm not dead," Si blurts. "I'm sitting right here." He grips Danny's arm with a shock.

"You're not in your body anymore," Danny says.

"But you see me," Si states quizzically.

"I'm a medium," Danny starts. "I've seen spirits all of my life. I didn't realize you didn't know at first." He hangs slumpily over the edge of the bed and says, "I'm sorry I didn't say anything sooner."

Si's eyes search the room for clarity. His mind twists in a storm of confusion.

"You're the first spirit ever to be ..." Danny begins. He searches for the right words to finish his statement. "This present? I'm not sure how to explain it."

"Danny—I don't ..." Si starts but pauses.

"I know," Danny whispers. He strokes Si's arm, trailing electricity on his skin.

"How?" Si waves his hand over Danny's magic trick..

"I figured banging my head has jarred something?" Danny reasons, "I don't know?"

"You're alive?" Si asks. His voice quavers, and his heart sinks. "But I'm a ghost?"

Danny nods, despondent.

"Do I just exist like this now?" Si asks.

18

5:38 AM

DANNY

DANNY SHRUGS. UNSURE WHAT to say. Spirits wander into his life all the time. He's a lightning rod for their energy, but never like this before. He's been speaking to spirits since he was a toddler. His mother did, as did hers, and all the women of his heritage.

He shakes his head, dizzy again.

"I've never had a spirit touch me before," he confesses.

Si rises off the bed and clamps his head in his hands. Trying to keep it from exploding.

Danny is suddenly aware that Si doesn't cast a shadow on the wall.

The sky is turning slate blue outside the window as daylight peeks over the horizon.

"What do I do?" Si asks.

Danny gawks for a moment. "Let's head back to the store," he says. "It's nearly time for shift change—we'll figure this out after that?" He doesn't know what else to say right now. It's not the first time he's had to tell a confused spirit they were dead, but Si is different. He's familiar in a mystical sense. "Si?" Danny asks, approaching cautiously.

Si turns to Danny with water eyes and wraps his arms around the clerk. Melting against him. His voltage surges right through Danny's body.

"Why am I just meeting you now?" Si asks.

Danny wonders the same thing. He peels back and swipes his thumb across Si's wet cheek.

Andalusite eyes glimmer back at him, longingly.

"What happens to me now?" Si asks.

"I'm not sure," Danny lies. "Just stay with me—okay?" he begs.

Si nods.

"Let's walk back to the store," Danny suggests. He reaches for Si's hand.

Si nods again, and weaves his fingers with Danny's.

"Don't let go," Danny says.

19

6:42 AM

"DEATH DOESN'T FEEL DIFFERENT," Si reports.

The city still smells like peanut butter cookies, and Danny still smells of apples and cinnamon toast. The flavor of the Hostess cupcake still lingers in his mouth.

His clothing still feels the same as it ever did, on his skin. The soft purple shirt flutters in the breeze while they walk. It all feels the same, even with the realization his body is just an illusion.

"Do I just keep existing here?" Si asks.

Danny looks up from the ground; his soft eyes have no answer. He squeezes Si's hand.

"I'm still here," Si responds.

Golden sunlight slips between buildings, casting its hue through the streets. Pigeons flit about the sidewalk, unmoved, and staring as Si and Danny pass by.

On the corner, two blocks ahead, a figure steps out from past the bend. She has wavy dark hair and a big familiar smile. Her long dress floats on the wind, even as the air falls still. She raises an arm to wave, causing the thick beam of sunlight, shown down on her, to strobe over the crosswalk. The golden aura around her glimmers as she retreats behind the building again.

Danny stops. His jaw hangs open. Staring ahead.

"Do we know her?" Si asks.

Danny doesn't speak, but moves forward. Pulling Si with him.

"Danny?" Si queries. He let himself be dragged up the sidewalk. His feet still touch pavement, while he feels as if he's floating.

"Mom?" Danny whispers. His pace picks up.

Mom? Si echoes in thought. *Oh,* right? *He sees spirits.*

A softly pulsating ache flows through their woven fingers.

"She's never visited me before," Danny whimpers.

They reach the corner, but turn onto an empty street.

The pulse reaches a crescendo and then stops.

Danny's eyes glaze over, and the ache is replaced with confusion.

"Keep going," Si says.

The convenience store is just around the next bend.

Danny trots forward. Tightening his grip on Si's hand.

Si's feet touch down and meet his stride.

Muffled voices bubble around the corner. Red and blue flashing lights reflect in shop windows across the way.

Police cruisers, an ambulance, and the coroner's wagon are mirrored in *"Divine Florals"* shop window.

Danny and Si pause in their tracks.

20

7:10 AM

"Oh," Danny says.

Delila shakes her head, pacing in circles, stroking and tugging a strand of curls fallen over her shoulder.

Two police officers and two EMTs huddle around her, taking her statement, with compassionate expressions.

A pair of men in matching slacks and ties cart a black body bag out of the convenience storefront and load it into the coroner's car.

"Danny ..." Si whispers. He leans onto Danny's shoulder and hugs his arm.

The knowing radiates from their combined aura.

"We both transitioned last night," Danny announces flatly.

He moves toward a bench, tugging Si with him, and they sit down to watch the show unfold.

Poor Delila is distraught.

Suddenly a crowd collects. People appear from doorways, corners, and thin air. Cars roll by, slowing down to be nosy, and then drive past. The city buzzes with its typical chaos.

Danny clasps Si's hand with both his, settling on his own lap, and squeezes. His grip is firm. Static. Magnetic.

"It's good to see you." A tender voice says from behind them.

Si whirls around in his seat. His face lights up as he says, "There you are." He hops up. "Danny, this is Nanny Grace."

The silver-haired woman with brown skin and kind eyes wraps Si in a tight embrace. She squints with joy and a broad toothy smile.

"I've missed you so much," Si cheers.

"I've been right here," Grace says.

"I know that now," Si responds, giggling.

"Hello, Danny," she greets, turning toward him as she releases Si. "I'm so happy you found each other again."

"Again?" Si puzzles.

Grace winks and says, "I should get going—you two have lots to do."

"We do?" Si asks, crinkling his brow.

"Yes, you'll see," Grace says. She turns to walk away. "I'll catch you again soon."

Danny looks both ways, up and down the street.

The coroner and his assistant drive away from the scene. A short while after, the police cruiser and ambulance disperse as well.

Delila gets straight to work, mopping the floor, and resetting the tipped-over end-cap of hard ciders, to prepare for another day.

"Hopefully, she'll remember to put that damn sign out from now on," Danny says. He turns to Si and adds, "I hope I've not left a horrible mess behind. She doesn't deserve that."

Si squeezes Danny's shoulder and says, "Let's go to the park."

21

BEYOND TIME ...

Si

DANNY'S EYES CONTINUE SEARCHING the landscape.

The river rushes under the concrete bridge. Water flows around its piles, causing a gentle sway of the structure beneath their footsteps. They cross over to Si's half of the city, hurdle the split-rail fence, and enter the park.

Birds sing for the sunshine, and squirrels scurry about the ground. The critters pay no attention to the ghosts, as the world carries on.

The gravel path still pops and crunches as they walk over the crushed stone. The air is still flavored, sweet and nutty.

"This is weird, right?" Si asks.

"Very," Danny responds.

The pair link their hands, with static current flowing through them.

Si studies the park and its inhabitants, carrying on with their lives.

A brood of children, with heavy packs strapped to their backs, walking together on the way to school. A businessman, toting his briefcase, marches long strides while huffing grumpily on his way to work. An old woman sitting on a bench feeds the birds fistfuls of seeds from a burlap bag. She smiles and watches Danny and Si pass by.

"How do we tell who's dead and who's alive?" Si asks.

Danny shrugs and says, "I've always seen spirits with a glossy sheen and brighter auras."

Si looks at the strangers again.

The old woman shimmers, reflecting warm light, like the sun on a hazy day.

"Why couldn't I see it before?" Si asks.

"I'm not sure we're supposed to?" Danny replies circumspectly.

The world around them blurs, like watercolor paint on a wet canvas. Colors bleed into one another, creating new hues, and then pull back to focus.

"What was that?" Si asks.

Danny shrugs and wiggles his fingers in Si's palm. "Stay with me," he says nervously.

"I'm not going anywhere," Si says soothingly.

"Good," Danny says with a smile. He steers them toward a park bench, facing a fountain with stone cherubs aiming bows and arrows that spout sparkling sprays of water.

He sits and invites Si to join.

Danny wrenches an arm around Si, holding him tight against his side.

Si nuzzles his curls against Danny's wild hair and exhales. "What do we do now?" he asks.

"I'm not sure," Danny says. His chest heaves, and he adds, "I've never asked anyone what this would be like."

Si lifts his head and turns to face Danny. He studies his profile. Subtle lines that crinkle the corners of his eyes disappear. His wild hair falls into order.

"You look different," Si says.

"I do?" Danny responds. He turns to face Si, and his eyes scan his face. Tilting his head, Danny says, "You do too."

Si kisses his cheek and hops off the bench. Breaking their connection as he floats toward the fountain. He kneels at its edge and gazes down into the reflective water.

"I think I look the same," he says and rolls his shoulders.

"You were already perfect anyway," Danny says.

Si trots back to the bench and pulls Danny up. He pecks his lips and says, "Let's go," pointing toward Park Row. "My place is just over there," he chimes, then asks, "Do you want to see it—before whatever happens next?"

"Yes," Danny replies without hesitation.

Their hands weave together, and Si leads the way.

22

SOULMATES ...

DANNY

Si's NEIGHBORHOOD IS THE polar opposite of Danny's side of the river. The sidewalks are pristine and sprout uniform rows of manicured trees that stand at the same height and in the same patterns as far as the blocks stretch. There's no graffiti on the sandstone buildings, and every street-level windowsill holds a planter box that likely blooms matching flowers in the summer months.

A busy cleanup crew of city workers wearing the same neon vests are already collecting the carved pumpkins from stoops, and "Happy Halloween" banners draped from cast iron lamps mirror both sides of the street.

The decorations on Danny's side of the river are more likely to wither in the natural elements and fall apart in their own time.

"I haven't visited this area in years," Danny says.

"How come?" Si asks.

"This place doesn't really care for my flavor of *riffraff,*" Danny replies. "Mom used to read tarot for the folks who live in these palaces." He ponders for a moment, then says, "Once she brought me to this incredible townhouse. Where she performed readings for this group of fancy adults—I was about seven, or so." His eyes light up at the memory. "They had shoved all the children into a playroom. It was full of toys and games I'd only seen in catalogs, or TV ads. But none of them really wanted to play with me ..." He lowers his eyes to the sidewalk, and continues on. "Except for one kid. This little boy with curly blond hair, and ..." Danny pauses and turns to Si.

Si meets his stare and lifts the edge of his brow.

"He shared paper and crayons with me, and we giggled as we drew funny monsters."

Si's face lights up, with that little boy's same andalusite eyes, blond curls, and luminous smile, now an adult.

Si gasps. "I remember!" he chimes.

Danny leans over and kisses his cheek.

Si stops the trek, tugging back on Danny's hand. "We're here," he says. He waves his arm toward the fire escape, which climbs to the roof of the three-story building. A white curtain flits out of an open window on the second level.

"Welcome home, my sweet boys." A voice sings behind them.

Danny whips around, and air catches in his chest. He swallows a hard lump and says, "Hi, Mom."

"Hi, love," she replies. Spreading her arms, inviting him into a hug.

He rushes in and wraps around her waist, laying his head on her shoulder, inhaling her scent. Warm vanilla and sage.

"It's so good to see you," she says, wiping his cheeks with her thumbs.

"Mom, this is Si," Danny says, turning and pulling Si closer.

"I know Si well," she says, smiling and shifting her eyes from one to the other. "It's about time you boys found each other again."

"Everyone keeps saying that," Si says with a chuckle.

"You'll understand soon," Mom says. Her eyes twinkle as she adds, "I love you both." She twirls fingers in tufts of hair behind Danny's neck. "Go ahead up," she says, nodding at the wrought iron ladder. "I'll see you again soon."

"Where are you going?" Danny asks, slightly panicked.

"Nowhere. I'll be right here—head up," she responds.

Si tugs Danny's sleeve.

Mom steps backward and disappears around the corner of the building.

The world blurs for a moment, and then focuses again.

Danny follows Si up the ladder and through the window.

"Welcome," Si says. He slowly spins with his arms spread out, then offers Danny a hand. "Come on," he chimes, and grabs Danny's arm, pulling him through the room.

"My entire apartment would fit in your bedroom," Danny says, chuckling.

"I love your studio!" Si elates. "This place is bland, you'll see." He drags Danny into the hallway.

Monochrome crown molding with a Greek-key pattern frames barely beige walls. One large painting, smeared with black and gold, hangs across from a doorway.

"That's the bathroom," Si says, waving dismissedly.

Danny awes the high ceilings and says, "You live here by yourself?"

"Yup," Si responds. "My friends live on the first and third floors, but this one is mine."

They pass through the hall, into an open-floor living room. The left half of the space holds a large U-shaped sofa, which faces a theatre-sized TV screen on the wall. Three massive paned windows flood light into the space. A magazine spread worthy gourmet kitchen with dark cabinetry and pale stone countertops fills the right side of the room.

"The spare bedroom is over there," Si says, pointing to a hallway directly across the way. He saunters into the kitchen and turns back, asking, "Are you hungry?" He pauses. "Do we get hungry?"

"I don't know," Danny replies and then yawns. "I do feel sleepy though."

"Hmm ..." Si hums and says, "Nothing feels different—shouldn't we feel different?"

"Maybe not?" Danny says with a chuckle. "I always wondered why some spirits didn't know they were dead." He sits down on a kitchen stool. "Now I get it," he continues, tracing a marble vein in the countertop with his fingertip.

A collage of memories fills his *knowing*. He stares at Si and recalls the boy he first met, and then the lifetimes that had been before this one. Always, blond curls. Always, hazel eyes. Always, the same big goofy smile.

Si nods with a dreamy expression and says, "Hey."

The click of a doorknob chimes from the spare bedroom.

A tousled ghoul waddles out to the great room, rubbing her eyes, and grimacing at the bright sunlight. She pauses, planting both feet on the hardwood floor, and surveys the apartment.

"Mallory," Si whispers, choking on the sadness in his voice.

Danny stares at her knotted bed hair and smudged Halloween makeup.

She looks through both of the ghosts, as if they're not in the room.

The phone in her back pocket buzzes, and she reaches back to retrieve it. Tapping it alive with her thumb. She reads the text message, pausing to absorb its impact.

Her face melts, and she rushes the phone to her ear. Waiting for a response.

"Hello?" The groggy voice on the other end of the line broadcasts clearly in the quiet apartment.

"Si is dead?" Mallory says. Then waits and repeats herself, as if she needed to hear the words to believe it.

"What?" the phone mumbles.

Mallory begins to cry. Her tears feel performative at first. Then she sobs and can't form more words.

"Si?" Danny says. Staring at the side of his face.

Si tilts his head, and his eyes glaze over. "She'll be okay," he says.

Mallory rushes out the front door, mumbling as she disappears into the hallway.

Si releases a heavy breath.

"Can we lie down?" Danny asks.

"Sure," Si agrees. His eyes droop, and he yawns.

Si takes Danny's hand and leads the way back to the bedroom. He kneels on the bed, and pats the spread, inviting Danny to join.

They cuddle into each other, and drift off.

23

ETERNITY ...

"DANNY?" SI CALLS OUT through a blinding-light void.

A sense of Danny materializes and responds, "I'm here—look at me."

His single dimpled smile and warm dark eyes appear, like emerging from a fog. Then, his entire face and being, present whole again.

They're both cloaked in airy garments from neck to bare toes. The light void melts away in an iridescent wash, and the space they're in turns into a vast dome. The indigo ceiling is like a night sky, sprinkled with glimmering stars, and swirls with celestial patterns like nebulas.

The floor beneath their feet is mirror-polished marble with iridescent veins that pulse a faint glow and reflect the glittering specks from overhead.

An endless stretch of pedestals stands in a line. Each holds a stone tablet.

The great hall of life records doesn't need an explanation.

Danny and Si both step up to the nearest pedestal, and a tiny pinlight appears. It dances over the tablet with a comet-like trail that carves their memories into its face.

Strange neon hieroglyphics form and dissipate, leaving the tablet blank again once complete. The pinlight follows suit, blipping away into thin air.

Danny and Si step backward and look at each other, smiling.

Si leans his forehead onto Danny's shoulder and releases a breath.

"Ready?" Danny asks.

Si nods.

The grand starry atrium fades away, and the bright void swallows them. They keep tight hold of each other's hands and slowly saunter forward.

The bright void blips and Si's ears echo with piercing rhythmic beeps. His mouth gapes open, but his own voice is delayed, until he releases a blood-curdling cry.

A giant, who reeks of ammoniated lemon, scoops up his body into their arms. The vile scent burns in his nose and throat. He can't open his eyes, and warm slime coats his skin until several hands scrub him clean with rough towels, only for goosebumps to coat him again.

He shivers until he's wrapped tightly in a soft blanket.

Continuing to screech, as he's laid onto a giant's chest and cuddled.

Coos and muffled voices are all around him for what seems like hours.blips,

They call him "Owen," repeatedly.

He recoils away when they attempt to shove a fleshy spirit into his mouth.

These monsters won't silence him.

Where is Danny? He wonders, unable to speak the words.

The giants pass him around to each other.

They keep calling him "Owen."

My name is Josiah! He would tell them if his mouth would form proper words. All that comes out are blaring wails.

Eventually exhausted and hoarse, he drifts to sleep.

Si, or *Owen*, isn't aware of how much time he's lost sleeping. *Where's Danny?* He wonders again. The first thought to cloud his panicked mind.

The room he's in is silent. He slowly pries his eyes open.

A smooth eggshell ceiling hangs overhead in the dim room. He's encased in plastic walls, and he can't move his arms, bundled tightly in the blanket.

Light filters in through gently swaying blinds covering a wall of glass windows.

He tilts his head, searching. Squinting until his eyes can focus.

Everything in the room is giant.

Where am I? he wonders.

A familiar static energy pulses to his left. It draws his attention magnetically.

When Si—Owen turns to face that direction, he encounters dazzling dark eyes, and a singular dimpled smile.

Danny ... in a newborn body.

Si coos, excited, and they both giggle joyously.

24

THE END . . .

Is only a transition

to what comes next.

Acknowledgements

Copy edits, contributor and advisor:

Lindsey Middlemiss

Creative friends and inspirations:

We are all static

and pure magnetic beings.

COMING SOON ...

Future titles by Michael Easton Star

"Notes of Orange Oil and Turpentine"
−2025

"The Wheels on the Bus Go Round" −2026

"Rations" −2026

"Hunch" −2026

"Birch" −2026

And more to be announced.

Follow the Star...
MichaelEastonStar.com

#Followthe⭐

www.MichaelEastonStar.com

FRUITBAIT
A Novella Remix
MICHAEL
EASTON
STAR